Hunger March

Hunger March

Secrets of a Dancing Girl

by
Cecily Riley

Hunger March

Secrets of a Dancing Girl
Book 6

Text©2020 Cecily Riley
Illustrations©2020 Emily Woodthorpe

ISBN 978-1-908577-95-5
ISSN 2515-1568

5 3 1 2 4
First Edition

All rights reserved

British Library Cataloguing-in-Publication Data.
A catalogue record for this book is available from the British Library.

Conditions of Sale
No part of this book may be reproduced or transmitted by any means without the permission of the publisher.

Although loosely based on related events, any reference to persons, living or dead, is purely coincidental.

Hawkwood Books 2020

To every naughty girl in this world

I am quite the stranger to despair. As a matter of a fact, I am known to always keep my cool and be ready to laugh along when the girls, the audience or Barnaby decided to be humorous. Hence, not only was I in the pits of despair but I didn't know how to behave or best to hide my unease. To top it all off, 1932 had seen a rotten October. It was pouring like mad. So, as I made my way into the dressing room and to my make up table that night, I felt like death warmed up - and looked it, too.

The reason for my uncongenial mood was that the souvenir Barney had left with me in June was starting to show. Not very much, but a trained eye like Mrs Huff's or Mrs Bartlett's would understand and start looking for a replacement.

I couldn't begin to imagine my life without the nightly shows, the girls, the fun, the freedom. That is why I was burdened with sadness and fear. I slowly started undressing that night, mulling over my predicament. It was all I could do to keep myself from collapsing in tears.

On the way to the theatre, I had decided, after long internal deliberations to get rid of the unborn child.

I had no intention of consulting with Barnaby over this matter. I knew his chivalrous nature would demand marriage and that he provide for us both.

I must admit, in my heart of hearts, there was little I wanted more than to be Mrs Cumberland, but I wanted us to decide freely when that should be and not when some reflex of Nature made us. All I had to do was find the right moment to ask one of the girls for a name and an address where my problem could be resolved.

I had no idea whom I should ask. I did not want anyone to know for fear it would weaken my influence amongst the girls and Mrs Huff. 'Only a careless girl gets into that kind of trouble.' I could hear her sermon already. Careless? She had met her husband at a time when showing one's ankle was considered pornography. What did she know? Golly! I was at my wits' end and I had a show to perform, including two tap numbers with smiles all the way through. I thought I was going to faint from the inner turmoil I was trying to control.

As it turns out, all the frenetic grinding of my mental wheels was wasted time: the answer came all by itself, unbidden. I was still standing in front of the mirror of my make up table, trying to look as discreetly as possible whether the bump showed under my dress. Absentmindedly, I was taking off my gloves, still staring at my waist in the mirror, when Jane's voice came ploughing into my consciousness. She was sitting next to me at her make up table with a hairbrush in one hand and a box of foundation powder in the other, her hair drawn back in a stark ponytail, her eyes bigger than usual, staring at me. Or maybe they appeared that way because of what she said next.

"Does he know?" she said, without a trace of scorn or criticism.

I immediately sat down, lest I would fall, and told her to shush while smiling all the time and leaning in close as if to inspect her foundation box.

"What do you mean?" I asked.

"Don't be daft. I would've never known but when a lass suddenly spends time staring at her waist, she's either not sure the dress was worth the money she paid for it or she's…"

"Shush!" I hissed.

"And that's an old dress you're wearing, much too late to ask for your money back… and just roomy enough to hide the…"

"Will you be quiet! Please!" I growled, leaning even closer to her so that both our reflections were in her mirror.

That's when I realized how drawn and pale I looked. I tugged at the dark bags under my eyes as Jane watched with a kind smile.

You're too clever to get yourself into that kind of trouble," she said with her delightful Scottish accent.

"Everyone thinks you're just tired… the girls and management. You're too clever to get yourself into that kind of trouble," she said with her delightful Scottish accent.

"But I have," I sighed. "I have indeed."

"You don't sound too chuffed."

"I am not," I said, turning from our reflections to her.

"But I thought you and that copper had something good?"

"We do, we do. It's just that: I don't think I am ready. I don't think he's ready. We've never discussed it. I don't know. I am so…"

"Calm yourself, love," she said, looking over her shoulder to make sure none of the girls had heard me. "You need to calm yourself," she said, putting her hand on mine reassuringly.

"I can't!" I whispered. Months of desperation were taking their toll.

"I suppose you'll be wanting to get rid of it then?" she said. "Do you know anyone?"

"No, and I don't know who to ask."

"I don't know either because I am barren as Bognor Regis," she said, caressing her flat tummy with a bony hand. I wasn't sure whether regrets were part of her statement. It was more matter of fact.

"What am I going to do?" I sighed.

"Don't worry. I may not know anyone, but I know someone who does."

"Who? Who? Tell me," I pressed her, squeezing her hand with impatience.

"Let off, will you?" she said, taking her hand away and shaking it. "You're not going to believe it but I really think you should ask Mrs Bartlett."

"What? That old spinster?"

"I know, I know, that's how all the girls think of her. But she's got a past too. How do you think she made her livin' before Mrs Huff asked her to boss us around?"

"What? She was working the street?"

"No! She was a dancer, just like us. And just like us, she got into trouble."

"She's always going on about virtue and being decent!"

"A hard-learnt lesson, I suppose."

"But aren't all the angel makers she knew dead? She's ancient."

"Not all that much! And I am pretty sure she still knows some of them," she said, giving me a knowing smile.

"What? Another girl asked you for help?"

"Yes, you're not the only one with a healthy body."

"Who was it? Who asked you?"

"I am not going to tell you!" she said, offended. "You wouldn't want me to tell others that you asked, would you?"

"No, no, of course not," I admitted sheepishly, ashamed at my nosiness. "Thank you, Jane."

"You're welcome, Lucy," she said, squeezing my hand. She looked up at the clock hanging above the door to stage stairs. "You just have time to catch her before she goes into the pit."

"She's here?"

"Yes, she always stays to watch the first few nights of a new show."

"I know, I know. I just thought she had been happy with what she saw yesterday."

"Apparently not," Jane said, rolling her eyes.

As our conversation drew to an end and I was feeling better about myself, I started noticing the world around me and the girls in the dressing room, as bubbly as ever. I had been so engrossed with my own life that I had only vaguely noticed Tina had run off - with Ron, astoundingly. In her stead, another German girl had been hired, Gertrud Müller. I saw what Mrs Huff had wanted to add to our group: she had large breasts, large blue eyes and gorgeous hazel curls. I doubted, however, that she had asked to speak or do anything other than dance for she was as dim as they come. Greta would have her hands full translating for that one.

I got up, quickly took off my dress and put on my dressing gown. I ran up the stairs to the stage. The audience was already there but it sounded like it was going to be one of the quieter nights. The stage hands were unexpectedly milling around on the darkened stage. They normally only came out of their green room when the set needed changing. As I made my way to the stairs leading to the administration wing, I saw why they were all on stage and all looked a bit nervous. Mrs Huff and Mrs Bartlett were having a whispered row with the new head carpenter, a Mr Doyle. They were standing next to one of the flats of the first number, "Cooking breakfast for the one I love". Apparently, it wasn't fastened well enough because when Mrs Huff shook that flat, the whole set wobbled. It was obviously not meeting her standards. Mr Doyle still had a lot to learn.

The reason why everything had to be so bloody perfect, other than Mrs Huff's sense of quality of execution of her designs, was that we had another star singer. It was a nuisance to everyone, beginning with Mrs Huff but it was a sure way for every show to be sold out that week. Libby Holman was our guest and she was going to sing two songs as we acted and danced that tune and also the central number with all the girls on stage, 'Auf Wiedersehen my dear'. It was the now obligatory German song in our show, not that any of us understood why Mrs Huff insisted on including one. She assured us it brought in customers and kept us on the good side of some of our more distinguished visitors. Only later were we to find out why it had seemed so important to win over our German friends.

At that moment, I didn't care a jot about the Germans, Libby Holman or the rotten set. All I wanted was five minutes alone with Mrs Bartlett and now it looked as if that was not going to happen before the fifteen-minute call. That was the time where I absolutely had to go change and put on whatever make up I had time for. I was running out of time for the operation and all too soon the stage manager would ring his bloody bell over the tannoy. For a moment, I toyed with the idea of going up to his little alcove and ask him for a few more minutes. I knew the old toad and I was well aware that he wouldn't budge.

I was just about to throw in the towel and head towards the stairs when I saw that the old women and Mr Doyle had come to some kind of agreement. He turned to his men and gave orders in hushed tones, lest the audience, on the other side of the closed curtain, should hear him. Mrs Huff and Mrs Bartlett were walking towards the administration door deep in whispered counsel, which meant they were quite surprised to find me standing there in my dressing gown instead of my costume, in street make up.

"Yes, Lucy, what is it?" Mrs Huff asked, quite irate.

"Actually, I had a question for Mrs Bartlett, about the steps for the first number."

"Your area of expertise, my dear. I gave you your usual table: in the back right corner, champagne on ice."

"Thank you, Agnes," Mrs Bartlett said, uttering a name neither I nor the girls had ever heard. But before I could wallow in the joy of having unearthed such a rare piece of information, Mrs Bartlett turned to me, a little weary. "Now, Lucy, I know tap is not your forte but you will just have to…"

"It isn't that, Mrs Bartlett," I said, not needing another lecture on how bad my tap dancing was or why it was the reason I was put at the back of the line in the first place. "I need your advice on a different matter altogether."

I dragged her away from the men installing extra bracing behind the flats, hammering as quietly as they could, holding her by the wrist.

"Yes, dear, what is it?" she asked kindly but taking back her wrist.

With that polite and kind question I noticed that, in spite of all the dancing and the bare flesh, her and Mrs Huff were two refined ladies with impeccable taste and manners. That's also when I realised I could confide in Mrs Bartlett and she wouldn't tell a soul.

"You see, Mrs Bartlett, I got myself into trouble."

"I am so sorry. What kind of trouble?"

"The kind of trouble that lasts nine months and then sixteen years before you're rid of it," I said, painfully embarrassed and glad that the gloom and blue stage lighting was hiding my blushing.

"I see," she said calmly. "And someone sent you to me to seek help?"

"Yes, someone seems to think you might know one of the women who does away with these problems before they have a chance to become…"

"I see, I see. Enough with the metaphors. Will you be so kind and tell that 'someone' not to send me anymore any more 'troubled' girls. I don't particularly want the authorities to discover that I know such people."

"I will, I promise. Will you tell me, though?"

She looked me up and down as if she was meeting me for the first time, as if we didn't see each other six afternoons a week for rehearsals, as if she didn't know me as the oldest girl in the line, the one who was always late.

"I suppose I could, but I have to say, of all the girls, you're the last one I expected coming to me for that kind of advice. I thought I noticed your footwork was even heavier these last few days and…"

"I am sorry, Mrs Bartlett, but I am desperate. The last thing I need to hear is how careless I have been and what high opinion you held me in. I am a woman, just like any other, capable of having children and happy in my love life. These situations are bound to happen. So. Will you help me or not?"

"Of course, dear. I am sorry to upset you. I know how difficult these times can be," she said. I was surprised to find that behind this demure and strict exterior was a woman of flesh and passion.

She gave me a name I didn't know and an address I was surprisingly familiar with. Who knew that such 'surgeries' took place in Notting Hill. I thanked her profusely and rushed to the dressing room. Just as my behind landed heavily in my chair, the fifteen minutes bell rung. As if the joy of having found a solution for my weighty problem wasn't enough, Jane and Rose, dragged over by my Little Mary, suddenly hustled and bustled around me, helping me to get ready on time. Jane put my shoes on, I tugged on my apron, Rose put the finishing touches to my make up and Mary adjusted the cap, attaching it firmly to my head. It had to hold up through quite an energetic routine and some had lost it in the process.

As soon as my little helpers were done, we ran upstairs and took our positions in the middle of the set that had hopefully been mended by now. The 'Cooking Breakfast' number included Rose, Jane, Ethel, Mary and I, all dressed as naughty housewives, slaving over breakfast. Although the song had become famous as sung by a man, the usual housekeeping norms were safe and sound at the Black Cat Theatre. Obviously, the skirts were too short, the shirts were too tight and we were much too happy to make breakfast. We danced and bounded around in that kitchen in a rather comical manner. The audience screamed, whistled and shouted so it had to be enticing enough. Our guest star for the week, Libby Holman, didn't seem quite at ease in this setting but put on a brave face and a bold smile. For a while, she attempted to sing over the racket our shoes made, walking along the front of the stage, back and forth. After the third call to get lost, on the first night she appeared, she retreated to the sidelines and let us gather the limelight and the audience's enthusiasm. She apparently had not been made aware what kind of show she was singing in or her agent had wildly misrepresented the atmosphere in our little den. Maybe the resistance to Libby's charms lay in that she was somewhat past her prime, at least compared to the leggy youngsters parading their assets around. Also, she was in between husbands and it didn't seem to agree with her very much. Or maybe it was just because her singing style was a little old fashioned whilst our show was decidedly modern.

The next number was 'Honeymoon Hotel'. Mrs Huff had had a rather original idea for that, modern one could say. She was known in the West End for her inventive ways to have us dance and let the skirts fly or have us still and starkers. The 'Honeymoon Hotel' though was very bold indeed. In the course of the song, Flora, the bride, was dressed by her bridesmaids Norma, Gertrude, Greta and Bridget. It was something of a reverse strip tease and rather lovely. Flora looked gorgeous in all that white lace, be it underwear or final dress. It was just an odd combination, sexy dancers and religious ceremony. By all accounts, however, I seemed to be the only one to find the theme bizarre. So, as my group and I changed with lightning speed into our travelling gear, complete with hats and suitcases, the second group merrily sauntered around the stage, getting Flora ready to say yes. Flora of all people! We didn't roam the same circles but I had cornered her some time ago, only to satisfy my curiosity as to what tied her to Ethel. She laughed at the question and told me they were only friends and parted as soon as they rounded the corner. She stressed that Ethel had not the same inclinations she had, it was only a mutual agreement for fencing each other's connections. When I asked what Ethel had to hide, Flora only smiled and put one of her white frail fingers in front of her perfect lips.

The next number, involving all ten of us, was again sung by Libby. 'Auf Wiedersehen my dear' saw us on various types of transportation. The set was impressive and the lighting just added to the drama. Stage right was an ocean liner's side in some exotic location. Palm tree cut-outs and a small hut was enough to suggest the South Pacific or some such place. Center stage was the front of an old steam engine train, complete with billowing smoke coming out of its funnel. That was a decidedly London set, with a lamppost and a bench. Stage left was the side of an airplane, the propellers slowly turning and a new dawn of adventures lighting it from below. These cardboard imitations were as close as most of us would ever get to real travelling.

We each came out of one of the means of transportation and went to kiss a designated counterpart. We then walked across the stage, miming conversations with our friend. Upon exiting, we would swap and we would re-enter on the other side, waving a white handkerchief at the audience with one hand while holding a bag or suitcase with the other. Libby sang in front of all the action, this number being less rowdy then the first one. The choreography of coming out of one and getting to the next one on time was tricky, especially since the second group had a quick change. Mostly it went all right and even if one or the other arrival wasn't greeted, it didn't matter to the audience, as long as there were girls in skimpy skirts strutting around on stage.

'Darkness on the Delta' took the audience to a sweltering night in New Orleans. I supposed most of them missed the specific location but everyone enjoyed this number. It was truly gorgeous, from what I was told and from what I gathered from the audience's reaction when the curtain rose. The set up was a nude tableau and the scene was a brothel, with girls in various reclining positions, lit by slanted lights only. Needless to say that, once we had rushed backstage and pretty much torn off our travelling costumes, we looked sublime, lying lasciviously in those narrow rays of golden light, on *chaises longues* and red velvet sofas. It was one of the 'sigh of relief' numbers, where all I had to do was lie there and look fabulous. Also, I was basking in the thought that I wasn't involved in the tap dance number coming up. Each night of that week I would have time to put on the curtain call dress, a blue overly sequined thing.

As soon as we had run off stage and the crew had set up the Indian camp, the other group came onstage in sparse squaw outfits, banging on little drums, tap dancing across the stage as if it was on fire. They did all that to the tune of 'Drums in my heart'. The girls smiled bravely and the audience went mad. Tap dance numbers were a huge hit with the men visiting our little theatre. The noise, the speed, the lunacy, no one knew why but it made them go stupid, shouting and hooting, dancing and hollering at the stage.

We could hear them well enough when we stood at the back of the stage, putting on our curtain call dresses. Afterwards, we had to patiently wait in the wings for the other girls to rush to the backstage and put on their dresses. When we were ready, the band played the standard closing tune and we came out, hands waving and hips swaying. Smiling more than our shattered bodies really wanted to, we walked along the stage's edge, in front of the closed curtain and collapsed as soon as possible, in our dressing room chairs. I don't why but this show seemed to be particularly taxing to all of us. Maybe it was just me and the state I was in.

I suppose that was also the reason why I had less patience with the after-show banter. They were all getting ready to go out but they were chatting, laughing and otherwise having a grand old time. I had a splitting headache and the stuffy air in the dressing room made me ill. I could feel Jane looking at me sideways as I sighed with annoyance. I wasn't in the mood to talk to her so she started the conversation.

"Did you ask her?" she said softly but directly.

"Ask who? Ask what?" I said, trying to let her know by the tone of my voice that I'd rather be left alone.

"Mrs Bartlett. You know, your little health bother," she said in what was probably her attempt at being discreet, though it only served to annoy me further.

"Yes, I asked her," I said, hoping that information would satisfy her and she would stop pestering me.

"So you know where to go?"

"Yes, I know where it is," I said, confused by her question, finally deigning to look at her. That's when I saw the sadness in her eyes.

"So you've made up your mind, then?"

"Yes," I said, downhearted by the turn this conversation was taking. "Why do you ask?"

"It isn't the simplest of choices. I mean, it's an important decision."

"What are you talking about? It's my body, it's my life. I am not ready to be a mum," I hissed, making sure no one was listening, feeling cornered by her questions. "And Barney doesn't know, so it's not his business. Plus, I am certain he isn't ready to be a father."

"Are you quite sure about that?"

"What? Yes, of course, I am sure. Why do you ask?"

"He just seems to really like you. How long have you been together?"

"A while. What does that have to do with anything?" I said, my turn of phrase becoming more curt under the strain of having to justify myself.

"It's just that, he's older than you, and he looks like the marrying sort. He might want to discuss it with you."

"Jane. Stop it. I know what I am doing. And Barney doesn't have to know anything," I said through clenched teeth.

Jane retreated to her make up table and that was the end of that conversation. I hurried up my preparations and left. The next day was going to be stressful and the day after that I would be exhausted, calling in sick and, in doing so, telling the truth for once.

As I walked down the drenched sidewalk, dodging puddles, I wished I didn't have to. I hated all the lying and I felt a touch of guilt about the life that wouldn't be. I wanted to keep dancing a bit longer before I turned into that scene in the show, 'Cooking breakfast for the one I love.'

***

I had gone to see the woman as early as she could see me. As a kindness, she had shown me into her 'parlour' before the sun had risen. I had hardly slept, I was too anxious about the surgery to find peace. Hence, I was able to call Mrs Huff around eight in the morning, staggering into the first phone booth I found, gladly resting my hot forehead against its cold windows. I knew she was at the office that early because she ran the theatre attentively and studied the books daily. I told her about an upset tummy and not wanting to spread the infection to the rest of the girls. At first, she argued that both I and the girls had seen worse. She must have heard some of my despair and exhaustion over the bad line because she didn't squabble much longer. She merely bid me rest and expected me to be back the following night. I thanked her and hung up.

The walk back to the flat had been an ordeal. My tummy was a riot of pain that my mellow monthly cramps had not accustomed me to. My legs were wobbly and my head was spinning from the ether. I suppose I should have taken a cab but my money would not stretch that far. With one night taken out of my wages and the healthy breakfast I had planned for the next morning, I had to make drastic decisions. Such a meal may seem too much of a luxury, given my situation but I needed something to look forward to when I felt better. At that moment, though, I felt rotten. I was sitting up in my narrow bed, the grey sky at the window might as well have been a wall. I was starting to reproach myself for the situation I was in, going over all the wrong choices I had made: going to that woman, not listening to Jane, not talking to Barney before it was done, asking Mrs Bartlett for help, working at the Black Cat and meeting Barnaby in the first place. I was going a bit mad but I had nothing to distract me from the pain and nothing to make it go away. For a very bizarre fifteen minutes, I thought the 'Angel Maker' had botched me up and I was, in fact, dying. Since I was still alive two hours later, I decided that Mrs Huff was right, I was tough and I was going to make it through that difficult time.

I felt so determined to feel better that I threw back the covers too fast and got up too suddenly. I almost fainted from the pain. I steadied myself with the bedpost, the chair and the sink until I stood in the kitchen. I had to have a cup of tea or the madness would start all over again.

The cold water splashed on my hand as I put the kettle under the faucet. It felt like fire and ice all at once. That's when I realised that, in spite of all my resolve, I had a fever. On top of a headache, I felt nauseous. I put the kettle on the stove and hoped for some kind of distraction. That's when I remembered the wireless in the attic of the theatre and the record player in the dressing room. Oh how I would have loved one or the other in my room, just so I could listen to a tune and dream of something else. A moment later, I was pouring the hot water into my mug when there was a knock on the door. It was a daily visit so I didn't bother to hobble to the door.

"Come in, Mr Spilsbury!" I said, staying at the sink.

"Good morning, miss," the round faced man said with a smile. "Here's the paper," he said putting it on the table like a precious relic. "I didn't do the crosswords, in case you wanted to do them," he said, blushing a little. "I took good care of it, for you."

"Thank you, Mr Spilsbury. It's so kind of you."

"Are you all right, Miss Lucy?" he said, hardly daring to come closer, as I was still in my nighty.

"Yes," I sighed and smiled. "Just a bit under the weather is all."

"I am so sorry. Would you like me to bring you a spot of broth?"

"Thank you so much Mr Spilsbury," I said turning back to my kettle and mug. "I need some rest, that's it."

"You're too modest, Miss Lucy. I haven't seen you this green around the gills ever. No protestations. Mrs Spilsbury is making shepherd's pie and I am bringing you some of the meat broth. See you in a little while."

"Thanks Mr Spilsbury, that's awfully nice of you," I said over my shoulder, too ashamed at my hunger and tears of relief to look him in the eye. "Give me two more hours of sleep. I can't thank you enough."

"Don't mention it," he said and out the door he went.

For no understandable reason, something released itself deep within my soul and I started to cry. I don't usually cry much but that morning I collapsed on one of our rickety kitchen chairs and sobbed and whined and wailed to my heart's content. I faced the sad reality that I craved someone to take care of me. I'd hardly had a mother, she had mostly kept away from me. On good days, she knew she was ill equipped to be a nurturing or steadying presence for a child. On bad days, she didn't know she was ill and took so many drugs, legal and illegal, that she barely knew I existed. So I was raised by a cold as a dead trout aunt, the same person who took me in when my mother was finally locked up in an institution, my father's death in the war not having helped matters. But, when I realized that my grey aunt's idea of educating me was beating me morning, noon and night, I got out of there as fast as I could. I had never known the warmth and comfort of someone holding and cuddling me. Until I met Barney, that is. And he was the one person I could not call for help. I let the despair wash over me for a while.

Having sobbed into my sleeves for a long while, the pain subsided, I ran my hands over my face and went to finish my cup of tea. I wasn't tired enough to go back to bed so I sat back down and looked at the paper Mr Spilsbury had brought.

POLICE CHARGE HUNGER MARCHERS the front page screamed at me with bold capital letters. Given the political inclination of the newspaper's owners, the strikers were accused of mostly any crime under the sun and the police had only made use of necessary force. But, even from the photograph on the front page, it was easy to tell that unarmed hungry men stood little chance against mounted, armed policemen. The scene at Hyde Park was quite chaotic and I felt glad, in an outlandish twist of irony, to be at home and nowhere near Oxford Street or Marble Arch.

The article was muddy as to what had started the riot. It made it sound like one minute the exhausted marchers were milling about and the next they were throwing rocks and breaking windows. With so many angry men assembled in one place, all of them convinced they were in the right, things escalated quickly. However, as this was England, public display of temper was frowned upon, no matter where you were born, Kensington or Glasgow. The protesters were soon dispersed and only one victim, a woman, was to be reported. Although a lot worse could have happened, given the circumstances, the person writing the article went to great pains to make that woman look like a sacrificial lamb on the altar of the marchers' selfish endeavour.

I was about to find out more about the woman as the reporter promised details below, when there were three loud knocks on the door.

There are very few people who actually made it to our bedsit on the fourth floor of Weymouth Street. I knew all of them and I also knew that the person outside that door was a stranger. I had been so engrossed in my reading, forgetting the world and most of my tummy pains, that both the intrusion of the world in my apartment and the presence of a stranger in my quarters made me quite weary. I was unable however to summon up a combative mood and stayed in my kitchen chair, telling whoever it was to come in.

I cannot express my surprise on seeing Charlotte enter, a little upset at having been left waiting. She moved quickly, taking off her coat and putting it with her hat and umbrella on the one hook at the back of the door. I was so amazed that I was thoroughly unable to move. So I watched her work in my kitchen. Her bony white fingers were flying over crockery and kettle.

"What are you doing here, Charlotte?"

"That is quite obvious. You are ill. I brought a few remedies and good tea."

She made a face as she poured the mug I had been holding in the sink and rinsed it.

"How did you know I was ill?"

"The women," she grinned, "they talk."

I was so dumbfounded by the whole situation that I took a while to make sense of what she had just said. It just wouldn't make sense. What women?

In the meantime, the beautiful old woman, standing in my miserable kitchen as if parading on the Mall, had pulled several pots and pill boxes from the carrying bag she had brought along.

"How do you mean? What women?" I blurted out as I inspected the suspicious looking powders she had put in front of me with a glass of water.

"Take them," she ordered, pointing at the medication, "and then, we'll talk."

It sounded like the kind of talk I wasn't sure I

wanted to have. On the one hand, I was dying to know how she had found out about my predicament. On the other hand, the few occasions we had met since June, it had seemed to me that she enjoyed taking something of a tutoring, nigh mothering role towards me. After a brief debate, I sighed, too tired to argue, even with myself, and caved. As I painstakingly swallowed what she had deemed necessary for the improvement of my health, I pondered yet again how little I knew about her. I was aware of the immense fortune and the incredible wit she possessed, and she always knew about every crime Barney and I were investigating. It was difficult to imagine why someone as regal as her would meddle with the likes of such criminals. In spite of all the admiration and respect I had for her, as I put down my empty glass with a sigh, I asked again what had brought her to my humble abode.

"I wanted to make sure you are all right, dear. And, as I know of your financial constraints and disregard for the medical profession, I thought you wouldn't have had the means or the inclination to get the medicine you need in your condition."

"I don't have a condition… anymore."

"I know! All the more important to take care

of yourself, should you want to find yourself in that condition again."

"But how? How did you know?"

"Now, Lucy, don't be so insistent. A woman is entitled to a few secrets and..."

"Exactly. That was supposed to be one of mine."

"You are being childish. I understand that you want to paddle your own canoe but you need my help. Plus, who am I going to tell?"

"It's not that," I started, but the tears welled up and the words choked me.

"Now, now, my dear," she said, patting my knee and putting an exquisite handkerchief in my hand, "I know, you didn't want me to know, you don't want your darling gentleman to know, because you believe we will think less of you."

"Exactly," I whined through my tears, clenching my fists hopelessly on my legs.

"I can't speak for your Barnaby but he seems like a reasonable fellow. As for me, I understand only too well the moral conundrum you found yourself in and how lonely you felt. I've been there. But I didn't have a young man's good opinion, not to mention love, to consider."

"What should I do? How can I tell him? Should I tell him? He doesn't have to know," I pleaded feverishly.

"Lucy, you're talking nonsense. Of course you have to tell him. You love him, don't you?"

"What does that even mean, 'love'?"

"My dear, I most definitely do not have the time to discuss the semantics of love with you," she said, getting up. "I just came over to make you a soothing cup of herbal tea, none of that black stuff for a few days, you hear? And to bring you a few tonics that should help you get back to work tomorrow… That Mrs Huff, she is tough, isn't she?"

"I didn't tell her," I said calming down a bit, wiping my face and blowing my nose. "Only Mrs Bartlett knows. And Jane."

"That sounds like a lot already."

"They won't tell anyone, I am sure."

"I hope so, dear," she said patting my hands, folded on the newspaper on the table. That's when she noticed what article I was reading.

"You shouldn't trouble yourself with such things," she said, sitting back down. "I am sure those ruffians are going to go home quietly after yesterday's fuss."

In spite of my ailment, my senses and instincts were still in perfect working order. They told me that something in her change in attitude was fishy. If I didn't know better, I'd be tempted to think she was telling me not to look into the riots at Hyde Park Corner. But there wasn't anything to look into - a large group of hungry men, an even larger group of coppers (one to seven, actually) and a few broken windows. And a dead woman. Was that what she wanted me to stay away from? Why?

I had the nagging feeling that Charlotte had watched my thought process because when I looked up from the paper into her icy blue eyes, I thought I saw her silently warning me.

"A fuss?" I said, feigning surprise. "It was a bit more than that."

"Of course, of course," she said, her defensive and tense tone telling me my suspicions were not unfounded.

"From the looks of it, it was a riot, quite unheard of in our time," I said, looking from her to the paper and back, teasing her.

"Nothing truly terrible happened. Surely a few broken windows and iron bolts…"

"A woman died, Charlotte," I said in a definitive tone. "That is truly terrible."

"I thought you'd grown less squeamish at the loss of life, dear. Really, you surprise me."

"I am not being squeamish. Someone died. And she shouldn't have. That is…"

"Maybe she should, and did, for good reason," she almost whispered, looking at me with a mix of shame and anger in her expression.

"How do you mean?"

I looked at her searchingly, the light coming through the tiny window above the sink insufficiently lighting her face. Her wrinkles and light grey curls belied a youthful spirit and a sharp intellect. I couldn't fathom what she had implied when she had said that the woman should have died in such terrible circumstances. There were no details as to her demise in the paper but something told me that my *vis-à-vis* knew a lot more than any newspaper reporter in town. She was quite relaxed now, looking at me as if she had been the one asking questions. The longer the silence lasted, the more guilty she appeared. In any case, if she had meant to distract me from my wobbly health, she had certainly achieved that. I was mesmerized by her secrets and her seemingly endless knowledge of London. In the spirit of friendship, as brief and heartfelt as ours was, and for the sake of getting things moving, I tried a different approach.

"A penny for your thoughts."

"You couldn't afford mine," she smiled.

"Oh, come on," I said softly.

"I am always amazed at how naïve you are," she said. "You have been sleuthing in the shadow of Barnaby for a considerable time and yet you still expect the simplest, nicest explanation to be the right one. How do you do it? How do you keep your faith in humanity?"

"You know what they say," I said, shrugging, "if you hear hoof beats, think horses not zebras."

"No, I didn't know that. How clever! So when you hear that someone has died, you immediately think poor, unfortunate soul?"

"Yes."

"Picturing the family who is going to miss her?"

"Yes," I said firmly. "You don't?"

"No, actually. I wonder instead what they did to find themselves in a situation that would cause such an unfortunate end."

"In this case, she might not have known there was a demonstration at Hyde Park Corner."

"Yes, I am sure one hundred thousand hungry men were easy to overlook," she sneered.

"I didn't know you had such a mean streak."

"Your comment was absurd and not thought through."

"You seem awfully confident of your poor opinion of her. Did you know her? Why did she deserve to die?"

"You do have a lot of questions, don't you? Are you sure you are still ill?"

"I am ill, but I am not stupid. When you dodge

my questions the way you are doing, I grow curious."

"I am not dodging them. I wasn't aware I had not answered them. Ask me again. What do you want to know?"

I was about to storm away with a barrage of questions, the same as before, but I stopped short. While it is true that I hadn't known Charlotte for very long, I was acutely aware of the width and breadth of the secrets she commanded. Now she was in my shabby bedsit, avoiding questions and looking smug. There could be two explanations for her behaviour: she either enjoyed teasing me or she wanted to protect me from the truth. That second option really frightened me because she knew I was accustomed to the crude violence of London's gutter. So far as I knew, she had never withheld information from me the way she did today. I was ill, yes, but how bad could it be?

"Tell me, Charlotte. Who was that woman? And why did she deserve to die?"

"Unfortunately, my dear, I can only answer the first question. The profession she had was… well… not legal, hence she used an alias whenever she practised."

"Practised? The article says she was in her late fifties, early sixties. Surely she wasn't on

Hyde Park Corner selling her favours in broad daylight?"

"No, dear, she didn't practice that kind of transaction. She took care of... well... the other end of that business, if you will."

"What? How do you mean?"

"Lucy, don't push me around like that. In your state, with what you've been through, I'd rather not say more."

"Oh but you will. I am well enough to hear this story. Spare me the polite riddles," I said trying to stand.

The sudden movement hurt and I bent over with a wince of pain. Charlotte put her arm under my shoulder to walk me to my bed. She helped me under the covers and pulled the blanket up. She patted my hand and smiled.

"Charlotte, please," I pleaded softly, "in plain English. What do you know about the circumstances of that woman's death?"

"Fine, fine, if you promise to sleep on it after I leave and not let that vivacious mind of yours run amok with what I tell you."

"I promise," I said, both of us knowing full well that that was not going to happen. Little did I know I was going to be kept up by a quite different distraction.

"The woman who died in the middle of the

riots yesterday might have been running from something, that is why she probably didn't look where she was going. She was probably clubbed to death by a bobby or trampled upon."

"You said you know where she was running from."

"Yes, that I know. You see, my dear, I manage a circle of women who help other women in their hour of need. That is how I knew I would find you at home, ill and bedridden. And that is how I know that the woman who died yesterday in those gruesome circumstances had performed the service, like the one you underwent recently, on a young lady in Bayswater. Unfortunately, that patient was operated upon by one of our less gifted 'angel makers'. As a matter of a fact, she made too many angels. In half her cases, the mothers did not survive her visit. That is what happened yesterday morning. That is how I am assuming that she was running south from Bayswater, quite oblivious of the gravity of what was going on around her."

I didn't know where to begin. I had so many questions. She ran an illegal abortionist ring? She knew that woman was incompetent and she let her operate all the same? As I should have known, I hesitated too long over which question to ask first. Before I could say anything, she had gathered her possessions, wished me well from the door and dashed down the stairs.

Her sudden departure and all that she had told me left me somewhat dumbstruck. I knew she had secrets. I never would have imagined that such a refined lady, no doubt the offspring of the English aristocracy, could be mixed up in such a sordid racket. Then again, I suppose her idea of a charity was to make sure who those 'angel makers' were. But why oh why had she let that one do her business risking young women's lives like that? I guessed she couldn't really control them or stop the inept ones from doing harm.

Suddenly, in hindsight, I felt terrified. I could have been operated on by one of those butchers. I made the decision there and then that, as soon as I was well enough, I would tell Barney everything and cherish every moment I had with him and ask him how he felt about us moving in together, sometime.

As it turned out, I was given the opportunity to test my resolve immediately. Without knocking, Barnaby stormed into my flat. He was obviously upset, which was worrying because he was a calm man. For things to get bad enough that he would lose his cool, they had to be bad indeed. He was panting, no doubt from the four flights of stairs he had just climbed. His hat was pushed back and his forehead was covered in sweat. His suit was neat but his overcoat was rumpled. He turned from the kitchen to the bed and was clearly surprised to see me lying down and awake at that time of the day. Usually I was either asleep or dressed and ready to take on the city.

"What are you doing in bed? And was it Charlotte I saw in the stairs?" he asked breathlessly as he came over hesitantly, taking off his hat.

"Yes, it was," I smiled. "What's the matter? You're so agitated."

"It's Auntie Kate," he sighed, dropping slowly to his knees, holding my hands, burying his sobs in the coverlet. "It's Auntie Kate. My God!"

"What's the matter? What happened?" I asked, puzzled by his behaviour, remembering this rather unpleasant woman.

"She's dead. They killed her!" he said, lifting his head ever so briefly.

I suspected nefarious people like her might live forever so I was surprised to hear of her early demise, and it took everything I had not to sound happy. Mostly I respected Barnaby's obvious sorrow.

"What?" I asked. "When? How?"

He sat on the edge of the bed and composed himself. He wiped his eyes and absent mindedly played with my fingers as he talked.

"Have you heard about the riots that took place yesterday?"

"Yes," I said, keeping my tone neutral but my stomach abruptly turning to brick. I felt a dreadful foreboding. I know where the story was going and I didn't like it one bit. I was immune to Auntie Kate's charms but being trampled by angry marchers was not how I wanted her to go.

"For some reason, she was in Bayswater yesterday morning. On her way home, she walked into Hyde Park Corner just as things were starting to heat up. Facts are still sketchy, rioters and bobbies are being questioned and arrests have been made. It's a mess."

I felt worse than ever. How was I going to tell him that I knew why she was in Bayswater yesterday?

"Surely, they know what happened to her."

"She was in quite a state," he said softly, tears choking him. "The coroner did his autopsy yesterday as soon as she was brought in but the examination of his findings is taking time. He won't know for sure until later today."

"Barney, I am so sorry," I finally found the presence of mind to say.

"Thank you, darling," he said and kissed me lightly on the cheek. "I know she wasn't the easiest person to get along with. Maybe I made it look like I didn't like her but I loved her like a mother. I owe her so much. She and Uncle Bernard took me in when my parents died. They made all sorts of sacrifices, when they didn't have to, so I wouldn't want for anything. And now this."

"Barnaby, I am so sorry," I said again, putting as much kindness and empathy as I could into those words, considering what Charlotte had told me. I was still trying to make that round peg fit into that square hole. Auntie Kate, the high strung, highly moral woman, was an abortionist! It just didn't go together, by any stretch of the imagination. While I was grappling with human contradictions, a storm was brooding in front of me without my noticing it… until I became aware of Barney's face and heard his question.

"But how about you, Luce? How are you doing? What are you doing in bed at this hour? Are you ill?"

Apparently, I had put too much sympathy in my face and tone because Barnaby had noticed something off. It had distracted him from his troubles and drawn his attention to mine. And now that he was there, asking me THE question,

I felt all my earlier resolve melting away like Icarus's wings. Let's face it, I was never going to fly as high as I thought I could. I had to say something before my hesitation became overly noticeable, and something that sounded believable.

The problem was that I loved him and I didn't want to lie to him. I also felt that if I told him the truth, he might stop loving me. I knew he had very high morals and principles. He turned a blind eye on my job because he knew that I was faithful to him. I didn't know how angry or sad he would get when he found out I took away from him the decision to be a father. Gosh, the more I thought about it, the more terrified I became. The silence grew. Something of my dismay must have shown on my face because the kindness receded slowly from his, to make way for a worried frown and, dare I say, anger.

"Lucy? What's going on? Why don't you answer me?" he said very calmly, staring at me.

"I will, I will answer your question. I just don't know how."

"We've been telling each other everything for the past five years. I thought we didn't have any secrets from each other, Luce. You're frightening me."

"It's not that bad, I hope. I just don't know..."

I whimpered. "I love you so much and I don't want to lose you."

"Lose me? How could you lose me? I am right here and I'll stick with you through thick and thin. I think I've proven that. I've put my job and my life in jeopardy to protect you. The least you can do is be honest with me."

"I do, I do. I want to be honest and I don't want to hurt you. You see, I…"

"Hurt me?" he said, getting up as if he had been splashed with cold water. "How could you hurt me?" He thought the question over for a second. "Is there someone else?"

"No! No, it's nothing like that. I love you and only you. You know that. That's one of the reasons why I've done it, so you wouldn't be pressured into anything."

He gasped and looked blankly at me. In spite of the deep anxiety I was in, I found space in my mind to admire how sharp he was. I could tell from his expression that he knew exactly what I had done. He was bitterly disappointed, then angry, but that cold anger, without noise. His face turned into a death mask and his voice became husky and monotone. I felt so dreadfully guilty and he wasn't going to let me off lightly.

"What have you done, Lucy?" he asked, his head lowered but looking at me all the same.

"Please don't be angry," I called, still lying in my bed, not afraid of him physically but dreading the moment when he would grab the door and never come back.

"I am angry, Lucy, as you can tell. Now, out of respect for me, I want you to tell me what you have done, that could possibly hurt me."

"I am so sorry you're angry, Barnaby. I wanted to discuss it with you but I didn't know how."

"Discuss it with me?"

"Yes. But then I, somehow, decided that it was my life too, my life first, and that that was the best decision."

"The best decision. What are you talking about? How is killing my aunt the best decision?"

"What?" I yelped in utter amazement. "I didn't have anything to do with that! I had an abortion!"

He turned pale and was silent. I suppose it was just too much for one man to go through in one day. He looked at me speechlessly, slowly backing towards the door. I am not sure he still could see clearly. Then again, neither did I. I was sitting in bed, the coverlet heavy on my legs, crying silent tears as I watched the worst possible outcome of my confession.

He tried to say something but his lips moved without sound. He slowly opened the door, his eyes never leaving me and, all of a sudden, he vanished down the stairs. I dove headfirst into my modest cushion and cried until I was exhausted and fell asleep.

It was dusk when Julia came through the open door, calling my name.

"Lucia, Lucia, what did you do?" she said, walking over to my bed, aware of the dilemma I had been wrestling with. "You did it, yes?"

Her catholic upbringing had featured prominently in the discussions we had had on the subject. I could now feel the whole of the Roman Catholic Church's recriminations weighing down on me. It was a heavy burden to bear.

"Yes, Julia, I did. I am sorry, I had to," I said, weakly reaching for her hand.

"Is your life, you do what you want," she said coolly, ignoring my hand.

"What time is it?" I asked as I saw the creeping darkness through the little window over my bed.

"Five o'clock," she said, going towards the wardrobe, removing her hat and coat.

"So late?" I asked, noticing how hungry I was.

Probably under the throws of unconscious ponderings over our fight, I decided that I had to go out and find him. The fresh air and walking would do me good. I got up and changed as fast as I could. Since that wasn't very fast, I had plenty of time to think about where to look first. His apartment or the Yard were all valid options but, knowing him, he would want to distract himself with work. I decided that my best option was to check in and around Hyde Park Corner for a tall and lovely detective searching for clues about the death of his dear aunt.

I snatched one of the slices of toast I had bought for my next breakfast and slowly walked downstairs. The fresh air did indeed help to clear the cobwebs. Very soon, sitting in a carriage in the muggy Piccadilly Line, I wondered why they thought Auntie Kate had been murdered. Who could have done such a thing? And why? She wasn't a charmer but killing someone because of their disagreeable demeanour was extreme by anyone's standards. Was it someone from the dead girl's family who had chased after her? Or was it someone who had used the riots as a cover to disguise his or her act? Or was it, as I suspected, really an accident? The coroner could be wrong. The wounds could have been misinterpreted.

My tummy was still upset and my little outing was stretching its patience. Then again, what was the point of a healthy tummy if Barney wasn't in my life anymore? I had to find him. I had to talk to him. I had to make him understand how hard and painful the decision and its execution had been. I so wanted him to forgive me, to love me still, to be with me when we both would be ready for a family. Just thinking about the possibility of him having really left me made me whimper. The lady next to me looked up from her knitting. I smiled at her. She smiled. All was for the best.

As I walked up the steps of the Hyde Park Corner underground station, I could feel something different in the air and it wasn't the dust still settling or the workers putting up boards over the broken windows. The traffic in Park Lane was normal for a Friday and Knightsbridge had its usual bus and cars comings and goings. Yet there was a tense silence, as if they were all driving by to pay their respects by a grave. Maybe it was my drug riddled, pain ridden, feverish state of mind that made it feel that way. Some parts of Green Park and Constitution Hill had been cordoned off. An impressive number of constables were milling about with large canvas bags, picking up what was left from the day before, maybe looking for a murder weapon. Others were standing at regular intervals around the cordoned off area, arms crossed, looking forbidding. But no one had a mind to walk onto that crime scene. The number of people arrested and the harshness of the police's response to the riots had put fear in the heart of the inhabitants of the capital.

I was taking it all in, leaning against a lamppost, resting whilst trying to spot Barnaby in the crowd of uniforms. As luck would have it, someone was going to take me straight to him.

"Miss Lucy! Miss Lucy!" I heard a friendly voice calling.

I turned and saw Constable Cooper, Mary's fiancé coming towards me, a canvas bag in his hand, quite empty by the looks of it. He was smiling, as if relieved to talk to someone and interrupt his back breaking work. I greeted him, trying to muster a smile half as warm and engaging as his. He noticed me staring at the scene over his shoulder.

"Quite the mess, isn't it?" he said.

"Yes, quite," I said, focusing on him again. "Such dreadful people."

"Don't be too harsh, Miss Lucy. They're hungry and no one's paying attention."

"I am surprised to hear you take sides with the marchers, Mortimer. What does Mary have to say about that?"

"She disagrees," he grinned sheepishly, "so I

don't speak my mind on the matter too much."

More lying or bending of the truth. Was that the real key to a lasting and smooth relationship? Was that the price I would have to pay to keep Barney in my life, obscuring facts and silencing opinions? It felt like a high price to pay. And then I spotted him, crouching at the feet of Wellington Arch, talking to one of the senior police officers, and it all seemed worth it.

"Do you want to talk to Detective Inspector Cumberland?" Mortimer asked, kindly.

"Yes, if that's all right?"

I got the feeling that Mortimer was a romantic at heart, a stark contrast to Mary's rigid pragmatism, acting like he wanted Barnaby and I to be together. He seemed happy to help to make that happen. He led me passed the bobbies watching the cordon and slowed his pace to keep up with me as we walked across the vast expanse of what was usually well kept grass. It was hard to imagine that only yesterday, so many marchers and so many more constables had clashed here. If it wasn't for the colossal amount of debris and upturned dirt, one could have mistaken it for an elaborate training manoeuvre.

When Mortimer and I stepped closer, Barnaby was alone, observing the ground. I felt Mortimer silently vanishing from my side. As much as I was glad to be close to Barney again, I would have appreciated his support a little longer. Here I was, exhausted and a little light headed from lack of food, but with an important, if not *the* most important task of my life to fulfil. I had to get him back. I had no idea how to go about doing that, nor what to say or how to broach the subject. I knew he knew I was standing beside him. Yet he kept his eyes down and his back to me. Maybe he was as hesitant as I was to start that difficult conversation.

Just as I had summoned the courage to speak, he stood and looked at me with the kindest expression I had ever seen.

"I deeply apologise, Lucy, for the way I reacted earlier. It was cowardly of me."

He took me in his arms and kissed me. I felt faint, from the relief and my general weakened state. But I kissed him back, as best I could.

"Thank you, Barney," I whispered into his ear as we held each other.

"Don't be silly. You have to forgive me. I was upset because of what had happened to Auntie Kate, but it is no excuse for acting the way I did, leaving you alone in that state. How are you feeling?"

"Not so good, actually. I am tired, but mostly I am hungry."

"I know a little pub on Brick Street. Come on, I'll help you. I am sure they can find us a bite to eat."

"Thank you so much Barney. Thank you for taking care of me."

"It's the least I can do," he said, signing off with a small gesture towards the senior police officer and putting his arm under mine and practically lifting me towards the pub.

We walked along Piccadilly in silence. I supposed the rest of the unpleasant conversation would wait until after I had had eaten. However, I knew the time was nearing when I was going to have to tell him what I knew about his aunt's demise. I didn't want to think about it and focused on holding on to him and cautiously crossing the broad avenue.

Down Street was dark and dank, like most of Mayfair. The pub was on the corner of Brick Street and seemed to have been there for a long time, with no aspirations of modernisation. I didn't mind as long as they served decent food. Barnaby deposited me on the window seat and went to the counter to order. There were only two other patrons and I blessed the silence and the gloom. It was terribly tempting to close my eyes and fall asleep, and that's exactly what I did, with the firmest intention of opening them as soon as

Barney returned. I don't know how long it took him to bring our order, but it was late when I opened my eyes to see the menacing sky through my hospital window. I was no longer in the pub! I lowered my eyes and saw the hospital bed and dormitory. Barney was sleeping on the chair next to me. Everything was startlingly white. If it hadn't been for Barnaby's dark blue coat and hat, I would have thought I'd died and gone to heaven. I almost did, actually. As my darling explained when he woke up a little while after me, I had fainted and he, having connections, got me to Great Ormond Street Hospital to be checked by a consultant. He said that recovery from the operation was going fine, that a solid meal was needed. For the moment, I had dodged the rest of that unpleasant conversation.

* * *

The following day I rested at the hospital and left so that I was on time at the theatre. I got through the show without panache but professionally. Barnaby had left before I woke up and I hadn't spoken to him all Saturday. When Sunday morning came I felt much better physically but uneasy about how I had left things with him. I had to tell him the rest of my story and make sure he was all right with those details too. A blanketing forgiveness was not enough for me. That morning, I had a quick breakfast and set out to Scotland Yard. I was wearing one of my beige ensembles, hoping to attract as little attention as possible. Since it was Sunday, things were usually calmer at the Yard. Apart from a few Saturday night ruffians and drunks, serious criminals seemed to take the day off. I suppose I should have known there was actually chaos at the Metropolitan Police Headquarters, since so little time had passed since the riots. But I was so focused on my little world and my big problems that it took me quite by surprise.

The noise, the agitation and the general atmosphere of disarray in the great entrance hall rather shocked me. The large space had standing room only. There were marchers filing complaints, families of arrested strikers wanting to see their men, constables with bandaged heads or limbs with very little patience for the visitors, journalists interviewing anyone bored enough to want to talk to them. It was a stark contrast to what I was used to. I had seen it very busy but there had always been an air of solemnity and control. It was not to be seen or felt that day. I got a little anxious, as if I'd woken up to find I was lying on barrels of gunpowder and the people around me were playing with matches. As I was weighing the pros and cons of staying, it occurred to me that Barney would probably have other things to do rather than chat with his girlfriend.

I stayed more out of curiosity than in the hope of meeting Barnaby. I started wandering the crowded hall, treading softly from one cluster of people to the next, gathering as much information as I could. I wanted to get a clearer picture of how things had escalated on that fateful Thursday. By the sound of it, the blame for the damage and fanning of the flames of dissent was going around quite generously, the bobbies blaming the marchers and vice versa. What was certain was that it was a miracle there had not been anymore casualties. The madness and disorder around Wellington Arch and all of Hyde Park Corner was hard to imagine. Identifying the culprit was almost impossible as the responsibility shifted depending on who I was listening to.

I was contemplating which steps Ramsay MacDonald and his government could take to improve these people's plight when I saw a group heading upstairs. The familiar energy of the tall man with the dark blue coat made me turn my head. He stopped half way up, gave brief orders to his subordinates and came over to me with a worried expression. In our little corner of the great entrance hall, a little way away from the crowd, the world seemed to shrink and we were quite alone. I had mixed feelings about this sudden *tête à tête*, one we had had before.

"My Lucy," he said softly, "what are you doing here? You were supposed to get as much rest as possible."

It may have been my agitation, but I thought I sensed a tinge of relief in his voice, as if he was glad to see I was looking so much better. I smiled at how softly spoken he could be about intimate things then so enthusiastic about others. But my mind was in a completely different place and I didn't remark on it. I felt shy and small again, as if he hadn't promised me absolute forgiveness in that hospital room.

"Lucy, what is it? Are you all right?"

"Yes, yes. I am fine. I just wanted to talk to you, in private, for a little while."

"I am busy right now, we have a witness list a mile long and we are conducting interview upon interview to find out…"

"Inspector! We have one you will want to hear!" a constable called, running down the stairs, looking me over disparagingly.

"I'll be right there," Barney said coldly to the constable, having noticed his disapproving glance. The bobby took off with a stiff back and raised eyebrow. "I am sorry, Lucy, I have to go. I'll talk to you later."

"No, take me with you!" I pleaded. "I want to stay. You know how bad I am at resting," I said running my hands under the lapels of his coat. "This will distract me, and I may be able to help."

His blue eyes were practically glowing as he searched for a solution to my unreasonable request. When he stumbled upon the answer, he gave me his broadest smile and whispered his plan in my ear. Once again, I was surprised at how clever he was, especially at solving my problems and indulging my many whims.

While he climbed the stairs to begin talking to the witness, hopefully stalling with the important questions until I joined in, I headed downstairs, as discreetly as I could, until I arrived at the lower floor. From Barnaby's sketchy indications, I was going to find the female changing rooms there, and sure enough, there was a door with a clear sign. I put on my 'I Belong Here' face and walked in.

I was relieved to find a rather deserted changing room. I made my way passed the four female constables getting ready for their shift, giving them only a passing glance. Once I was out of sight, behind a row of lockers, I tried a couple of lockers, trustingly unlocked, opened the door and held the uniform against me which fitted reasonably well. I got changed as quickly as possible, but that uniform was no cabaret costume. The black serge fabric, shoulder pads and golden buttons made it dreadfully unwieldy. All the same, I came out into the empty corridor looking the part. I held my clothes in a bundle under my arm, keeping my quick exit options open.

With a very straight back and a stern expression under my black cap, I went up the stairs to the offices and interrogation rooms. Barnaby had given me the number of the room in which he was working that day, but I still needed an excuse to be let into the room. The day was so chaotic that, unlike any other day at the Yard, all the interrogation rooms were busy, and all their doors had a constable keeping watch. I walked confidently down the corridor barely containing the agitated crowd of suspects, witnesses and representatives of the Metropolitan Police. I made my way to Barney's interrogation room. I grumbled something about being 'sent from upstairs' and an 'essential message' to the colleague at the door and was let in. Barnaby looked up, quite ready to tell off whoever had interrupted his conversation but stopped himself just in time on seeing me.

"Yes, constable, what is it?" he asked curtly.

"The new evidence you asked for," I said in the same professional manner, handing him my bundled clothes.

"I didn't know they would be delivered here. A report of the specialist's findings would have been better," he said, as if chastising me for the poor idea.

"I know, I am sorry, Detective Inspector. There was some mix up in this case," I said, looking at the witness sitting across from him.

He was a heavyset bobby in his mid thirties with black curls and proud sideburns. His expression suggested that while he may not have been the cleverest copper, he was not totally unobservant.

"Since you're here, you may remain and take notes," Barney said disdainfully, returning the bundle to me.

At any other time, I would have had a thing or two to say about his condescending tone or the role he gave me, but it was an act, and a decent one. I looked for a pencil and small notepad in my uniform and made like I was ready to start writing.

"Now, Constable Gray, where were we?" Barney said, with a much warmer tone, to his colleague.

"We had just started moving forward, to keep the marchers from getting any closer to Buckingham Palace, shifting the crowd towards Hyde Park. I was on foot, in the front line, with the other lads on either side and the mounted division spread thin behind us. Now, Inspector, I know the marchers and what they look like. They came from all over the country, tired, dirty, hungry. Those who didn't belong there stuck out like a sore thumb."

"Those who didn't belong there? Who do you mean?"

"Some of the local lads, who were there to make trouble, blokes with darkness in their eyes and a lust for blood."

"Let's try to remain as factual as we can and not get carried away. You make them sound like mystical creatures. You mean they were ruffians?"

"Yes, but looking to make trouble, without a cause, certainly not there because they wanted to support the marchers, or if by support you mean make a nuisance of themselves, by lashing out at us for instance."

"And you were there when this whole mess

started?"

"Yes. The marchers were quiet enough, grumbling and bored mostly. Then the boys from Marylebone, you could tell they were from here because they were better fed and the clothes were cleaner, started shouting at us. Nothing much at first, rallying slogans, you know. But then it grew progressively worse, the language, you see, Inspector. They started name calling. We knew we had to stay calm but they were nasty and nagging, like the wife at home, you know?" he joked.

"No, I don't know," Barnaby said, ice cold, decidedly not looking at me. The bobby wiped the smile off his face.

I stood against the wall, between two bobbies who were far too engrossed in the narrative to notice me or my name tag.

"Sorry, Inspector, I meant that they were trying to get under our skin, you know? I am sorry to say, they managed that all right. Fisticuffs and boxing matches broke out amongst the marchers and some of the lads got their batons out and tried to keep the roughest from moving forward. I was very busy keeping the peace and taking some of them down when I noticed a man who had no business being there. Many of them didn't have any business being there, but he really looked out of place. In the middle of wrinkled shirts and cheap trousers, workers caps and dirty hair, I saw a well-dressed man, a gentleman you might say, well passed sixty years old, in a tweed jacket and pressed light coloured trousers. He had pomaded hair and could have lost a few pounds. He looked worried, because of the noise and the commotion I suppose, but he kept going, he kept moving towards the thick of it."

Now I was engrossed, too. Who was that man? Constable Gray was a formidable teller of tales. I could have listened to his stories all day. I think all four of us held our breath for what came next.

"I wanted to catch up with him, tell him that things were going to get ugly and that he should go back home. He seemed to spot someone in the crowd and moved even towards Wellington Arch. He vanished in the crowd, just as the shouting was getting deafening and some of the marchers turned on us. I didn't have time to think about him anymore."

The constable continued with extraordinary detail, lists of names and injuries incurred by both sides. It gave me time to think about that mystery man. Who was he? What was he doing in such a place? Did he know one of the workers?

Did he want to keep that person out of danger? In a moment of clarity, two thoughts collided in my brain. First, I remembered that that was where I had found Barney the day before, at the feet of Wellington Arch. Could it be coincidence? Or was it the spot where Auntie Kate had been found? Had I seen him pick up some reddish sand and put it in an evidence bag? I had been distracted by my tummy cramps and Mortimer's banter. I had stared at him all the way from the cordon to the arch, but I didn't consciously register what he was doing. I was drugged and in love, two of the best reasons not to pay attention to the gruesome details of a possible murder scene. But now that I was feeling better and thinking clearly, I remembered him crouching there, forlorn and lost.

The other thought was more of a hypothesis or at most a random guess, and even more disturbing. As I remembered Constable Gray's description of the man, it reminded me of someone. I am aware that we all perceive people a little differently, which means that I would not necessarily describe a person the same way a policeman in the middle of a riot would. Feminine intuition versus police experience and so on. But from the details given by Gray, I thought of someone very specific, someone who knew the victim well. Hence, my question might find an answer in the circle of people I knew, a legitimate supposition since I knew the victim. As a matter of a fact, if the victim knew the murderer, the Inspector sitting in front of me knew him, too. I wondered if Barnaby was drawing the same conclusions. I would have given my last penny to see his face but I had to stand there and wonder if he had recognised the man in the constable's description, as I had. I couldn't do anything at that point, so I pushed away the thought and tried to concentrate on the rest of Gray's interview.

"Things were getting quite out of hand, Inspector, let me tell you. There were fights breaking out left and right, with the crowd movements we had feared. Some were fleeing the confrontation, others were coming to the wounded's help. It was topsy-turvy. I stood my ground as best I could."

"I am sure," Barney said coolly. "Carry on."

"There I was, trying to keep my head when I saw that posh old man again."

"Yes?" Barney asked, interested. "Which way did he go."

"He was staggering. At first, I thought he was wounded because of all the blood, you see?"

"What blood?" Barnaby asked, raising his

voice but a little.

"I don't know, inspector. There was too much confusion for me to reach him. He kept walking as if he knew where he was going, not caring a jot about the pandemonium around him. He was going in the opposite direction this time, down Knightsbridge. Other than the blood covering his hands and some of his shirt, his face looked changed. On the way in, he had been nervous and agitated but he had looked liked a jolly chap, the kind of man who enjoyed an armchair and a pipe. On the way out, he was hurrying, and pale as a sheet."

The story continued but I was so distraught I couldn't listen. I don't know how Barney kept up appearances. Unless I was very much mistaken, Barnaby knew the 'jolly' man, probably better than anyone on Earth, bar one. Hence it must have been even more challenging for him to ponder how the quietest, gentlest man could walk down the street with blood on his hands and the death of a woman on his conscience. There were so many fountains in London, he had no doubt cleaned himself up before taking the underground to Fulham Road. Or did he walk all the way to his front door in a daze, not quite understanding what he had done? I had read that dramatic circumstances could make people do unbelievable things.

"That's when we ran the last ones off, Inspector," Gray continued. "We started cordoning off Duke of Wellington Place and…"

"Thank you, thank you, Constable Gray. That will be all, you can go back to your duties now," Barney said, tonelessly. The other two constables followed him out.

"Miss, you can close the door, we will go over your notes," Barnaby said, for the benefit of the three men exiting, although it had been very obvious that I hadn't written a word. All the same, I closed the door behind them, shutting out the noise coming from the bustling corridor and sat down across from him. He was ashen faced.

"Barney? Are you all right?" I asked, putting my hands on his. That seemed to raise him from his stupor.

"Yes, yes, I am fine."

"What, what do you make of what Constable Gray said?"

"What do I make of it?" he asked. "What do you make of it, Luce?"

I was unable to tell if his dazed tone and expression indicated the coming of rage or despair, so I trod carefully.

"Do you not know in your heart who that 'jolly' man was?"

"Yes," he said coolly, "and so do you." I remained quiet. "Who that man was," he sighed. "It seems so obvious and so unbelievable all at once. I am just glad Constable Gray and the rest of the lads have never met my family because... Lucy, let's face it, even if they had only met Aunt Kate, they would have recognised her on that slab of marble downstairs. Then the questions would have been directed at me and not the other way around."

"You haven't told them that you and the victim are related?"

"No! And I am not going to, especially not now that a man matching Uncle Bernard's description is the prime suspect."

And there it was.

"Goodness, Barney! Do you really think it was him?"

"By God, I hope not. I don't know what to think."

I felt so sorry for him, such a fair heart in a foul world.

"Maybe we could go and talk to him, together, tomorrow?" I suggested.

"Tomorrow? Why not today?"

"I am going to be late for rehearsals as it is and although Mrs Bartlett is understanding about my circumstances, there's only so much leeway she's willing to give me."

"Of course. You go now and I'll pick you up tomorrow on the dot of nine."

I kissed him, grabbed my bundle of clothes and flew down the stairs, ignoring calls from the superiors of the person whose uniform I was wearing. I grabbed the first cab I found, my own clothes safely tucked under my arm.

I was only five minutes late when I emerged at the top of the dressing room stairs, and quite proud about it, too. That feeling was not to last. The atmosphere awaiting me at the theatre was that of suspicion and whispers and stolen glances in my direction.

"Miss Lucy," Mrs Bartlett cut through my paralysing dismay and the other girls' chatter, "how good of you to join us. Now, ladies, if it's not too much trouble, please line up and let's see what your night has left us with."

We lined up reasonably quickly, but there seemed to be something of a void around me. As Mrs Bartlett took us through the warm up exercises, I stole glances towards the rest of the girls, in front and behind me. Jane looked at me kindly enough but the rest of them were definitely giving me the cold shoulder. Even Mary, with whom I'd been having good talks after the show over the last weeks, stared blankly as if she didn't know me. I couldn't wait for the refreshments break to find out if the problem was indeed the decision I had made. Even if it was, their collective reaction frightened me. Since I am not one to back down from a fight and knowing I had wronged none of them personally, I was ready to confront them.

The water break, however, provided no such confrontation because Mrs Huff came down from her office to give us a little pep talk and explain what she had put together for the next show. Greta translated as best and as fast as she could for Gertrude, who was to become Gertie very soon, which she enjoyed immensely. Other than that, the girls were quietly listening. I felt no animosity coming from Mrs Huff as she looked at me on her way out, so I assumed she either didn't know or didn't care, as long as I was up to scratch every night from now on. I was a little relieved as I turned to a group of hostile looks, but nothing came of it because Mrs Bartlett called for the rehearsal to continue. We danced until she declared our efforts passable and let us return to the dressing room.

I was apprehensive of what awaited me in that bear pit. I followed the other girls down the stairs slowly. They were all eerily quiet in various stages of prepraration. I stood on the last step overlooking the two rows of make-up tables on with their lit mirrors, two railings of costumes in the middle and the exit door at the opposite end. I couldn't remember the last time it had been this quiet. The discomfort was starting to eat at my insides, which were not entirely healed and had disapproved of this rehearsal vehemently. All the same, I couldn't leave things the way they were. I had nothing to feel guilty about, but this atmosphere was unpleasant for everyone. I blurted out, at no one in particular.

"Well, what is it? What's the matter?"

"Why should anything be the matter?" Ethel sneered into her mirror at my reflection.

"Jane," I said, going to her for help, "what's going on?"

"You leave her out of it," Bridget cried loudly from behind the railing, her Irish accent thicker in her agitation.

Some of the girls stood up to watch what was about to unfold. I was face to face with Bridget, half the girls behind her, the other half behind me. Jane sat between us. Needless to say, she looked ill at ease.

"Keep her out of what?" I asked as I saw our favourite Dubliner's face turn as red as her curls.

"At least, she had the decency to tell us," Flora said as haughty as ever, leaning against the door frame of the stage stairs.

"Tell you what?" I asked as I looked down, searching for Jane's gaze.

It was only when I saw her usually proud stare falter that it dawned on me. Someone had been a tittle tattle. I had to let that sink in before I could face my accusers with a semblance of strength. Jane's expression seemed to show deep hurt and confusion. What was the point of being angry at her? It had to come out sooner or later.

I stared out Bridget while focusing on my breathing, to stay calm and keep control.

"How could you?" Bridget opened, in the grand tradition of overly dramatic questions.

"How could I what?" I asked, bored already with the moralistic gibberish that I knew was coming my way.

"It's a sin, don't you know that?" Bridget said with the same tone she would have used to ask me if I knew the Earth was round.

"I don't go to church, I don't believe in God but it is a woman's right to choose what happens to her body."

"It wasn't just your body, was it?" she hollered at me, inflated with self-righteousness.

"It was mine, yes. And none of you have any right to judge me. None of you! If and when I have a child, I will want to give it the best possible chance in life. That is not something I can do right now."

"The gift of life is not one you can send back," Norma said, a lot calmer that Bridget.

"It's not a gift. It's a biological result that has existed for millions of years, no more. Since we are no longer cave women at the mercy of others, we can choose whether or not to accept that result."

"God forbids…" Bridget started.

"Bridget, if you keep quoting the bible, written by men I might add, filled with ancient, outdated rules, laws and morality, I will have to punch you," I said, quite out of breath and at the end of my patience.

"Not if I punch you first," Bridget shouted.

Mary and Rose stopped Bridget in the nick of time whilst Norma and Greta held me back.

We were lashing out with words, raining down insults on each other. Poor Gertie got more than an earful of colourful new English words. Since my time in the gutter had not lasted as long as Bridget's, I lost the mud slinging banter, but I wasn't giving up without taking a few of them with me.

"You know what, Rusty, you and your principles can go hang. Half the girls in this room have done the same thing with their `gift`," I said by way of conclusion, shaking off my female restraints.

"What?" Bridget said, looking around at the girls' faces as if she had just discovered she was standing in crocodile infested waters.

Rose, Jane, Ethel and Norma looked a little embarrassed, but we had no time to dwell on spreading blame because heart wrenching sobs erupted behind me. I turned with a knot in the pit of my stomach, forgetting all about my anger and demands for understanding, feeling nothing but dreadful sympathy for those tears. I was truly worried because I knew who was crying thus and she never cried in public. She never displayed extreme mood swings of any sort. I knew that if she was crying like that, in front of us all, it must be bad news indeed.

Before anyone could do anything, I took Mary into my arms, letting her sobs subside on my shoulder. The other girls' states of mind were a mixed bunch of physical tiredness, emotional exhaustion and general wonderment. They shared compassionate glances towards us then resumed their seats. They knew how Mary shared little of her personal life and how protective I was of her. They started softly chattering amongst themselves. I got Mary to sit down in her chair, between Rose and Ethel. I whispered the standard reassurances to her since I did not know what the matter was. I crouched in front of her, holding hands in her lap. I gazed deep into her blue eyes, ever so slightly reddened by tears. She was quite calm now, even if very sad still.

"What's the matter, Mary?" I asked, suspecting that it was related to Mortimer, but I couldn't or wouldn't imagine what he had done to have her cry like that.

"It's Mortimer," she said softly, confirming my thoughts as if confessing a cardinal sin. "He... we... I can't have children."

I was shocked, truly struggling with the notion of infertility so close to my resolved predicament. Then the next surprising implicit fact hit me. "But you two aren't married."

"We plan to be," Mary whispered, turning deep crimson, "in April, but this! And you two are arguing about abortion!"

She started sobbing again. I could feel Ethel's glare on me from above. Rose had gone for a pre-show dinner date. She had found some manner of fame at the Black Cat. I wondered where my carefree days had gone, and remembered that they hadn't been carefree for long. My giddy and light-hearted demeanour was a front I brought out if I wanted to shine on stage and keep working.

Flora almost kneeing me in the back brought me out of my daydreaming. She and Ethel, ready for the show, fled to the opposite corner of the dressing room to chat, no doubt about me. I looked around for a handkerchief. Mary thanked me and finished preparing herself for the performance. I sat down at my make up table and applied the stage paint, trying to forget all about the drama that had passed.

After the show, which had been excruciating, I slowly walked downstairs amidst the girls' usual chatter. I sat down with relief and meticulously took off the curtain call dress. I would probably be the last one out, burying any plans of seeing Barney that night. Then again, given the early and important interview we had planned the following morning, it was probably best if I went to bed as early as possible.

Norma was putting the final touches to her make-up when she noticed me staring blankly at my hands on the make up table. She pulled her chair across the corridor right next to mine, a sudden and intimate presence.

"Hello Norma, how may I help you?" I said responding to her inquisitive gaze and eager smile.

"Thanks for not naming names," she said.

"You're welcome," I said coolly. "Was there anything else?"

"Yeah. I've heard that you're working with your cop friend on the death of the old lady at the riots."

"How do you know that?" I asked, taken aback.

"We have a common friend, the lady who helps 'careless' girls like us."

"You mean Charlotte?" I whispered so low, I was surprised she could hear me.

"Yeah, yeah. So? What's the buzz?"

"The buzz?"

"The buzz, the chatter, the lead the two of you are following up?"

"I can't tell you that."

"Come on, you can if you want to."

"I could but I won't. Besides, I don't know a thing."

"You got your answers mixed up, honey! First you deny knowing then you argue why you can't talk."

"It's all the same to me. I can't and won't tell you a thing."

"That's too bad," the American said, looking downbeat.

"How come you know so much?"

"She's the one who 'worked' on me, and I

almost died. Charlie found me and took me to a real doctor and paid for my bills, too. For a few days, they didn't know whether I was going to pull through."

I was appalled and said so, starting to grasp the horror of all that had happened. Auntie Kate, due to her incompetence, might have had several girls' lives on her conscience. It didn't matter to her anymore, of course, nor to those who had died while in her care, but the living would want to know that some kind of justice had been done.

Or had it?

I couldn't wait for the night to be over and to be on that sidewalk, waiting for Barney to pick me up so we could question Bernard. I said rather abrupt goodbyes to the room and left as soon as I had changed.

My tiny bed and cold bedsit were calling me.

* * *

Next morning, I came downstairs anxious about what had to be done but eager for adventure. I liked Uncle Bernard and feared what conclusion the day held for him. I had, however, been hampered by my health for the last few days, a handicap I was quite unaccustomed to and I was getting impatient with it. The planned interview was a welcome change of pace. Unfortunately, a disappointing message was waiting for me in our mail box. Beside a letter from Italy for Julia, there was a note from Barnaby. Since it was devoid of a stamp and only bore my first name, I had to assume that Barney had dropped by some time in the evening to leave it for me. For a moment I feared that the entire excursion had been cancelled but when I read the note, I was reassured. Barnaby simply asked that I join him at the Yard so we could go together from there. There was every chance that the events of the past few days kept everyone very busy at Victoria's Embankment, with thousands of complaints being filed for police brutality, instigators being investigated for disturbing the peace and witnesses for both sides being questioned.

Certain that Barney would foot the bill, I hailed a cab on Portland Place. They had become a lot more numerous in our neighbourhood since the BBC had inaugurated their new building. On the ride there, I wondered in what state we would find Uncle Bernard. Would he confess? Would he lie? Would he be surprised? Those questions would be answered closer to lunchtime than I had expected, but, for now I was keen as mustard, driving in a cab across London, going towards my love, another adventure and hopefully the discovery of a truth close to my heart.

At the Yard, I asked the cabbie to wait for me and briskly walked across the frosty sidewalk. Being at Scotland Yard, he hardly thought I would be cheating him and readily agreed. Although it was only the end of October, winter had come early, or so it felt that morning. The stress and agitation had ever so slightly lessened in the great hall of the Metropolitan Police Headquarters. It was the same collection of plaintiffs, culprits, suspects and bobbies but somehow the noise level was almost back to a tolerable level.

I looked around the faces in the great mass of people coming and going on the hard marble. As I failed to see Barney, I reluctantly joined the dishearteningly long queue in order to speak to someone at the counter.

I wondered what business had brought them to this place on a workday. Most of them being unemployed, I guessed they had no better place to go. It was in that state of advancing boredom, static queuing and cab bill rising that Barnaby found me, breathless, blue eyes sparkling.

"There you are," he said as if I had been

hiding all this while. "Are you ready to go?"

"Yes," I said, stepping out of the queue, "the cab is waiting outside."

"Good girl. Let's go," he said, putting his arm around my waist and pushing me towards the exit, "no time like the present."

"Has any more evidence come to light?"

"Regarding our suspect? Not really. Another constable may have seen the victim pass him by near Park Lane."

"He remembered a single woman in all that crowd?"

"There were only men at that gathering, remember? A woman would have been noticeable."

"Then why didn't anyone else see her?"

"The bobbies were too busy controlling the crowd," he said with a slight nod towards the hoardes of people.

"And him? No one else saw him arrive or leave?"

"I admit, he was vastly different in age and dress than most of the marchers, but he was still just another man at the Wellington Monument which is in the middle of the green, the furthest point from any police force at the time."

"Has no marcher come forward to give his account of what happened at the Arch? Surely someone must have seen something."

"Apparently, the marchers have various other bones to pick with the Met right now," he said, helping me climb into the cab, giving the driver his uncle's address.

With that, he sat back and watched the buildings pass us by while I stared at the Thames, worrying how the upcoming interview would affect him. I had only just started picturing the options of what could have happened in the middle of the riots when the cab slowed to a stop. The driver swore and Barnaby murmured, "Here we go".

I looked at the road over the driver's shoulder and the sight frightened me. Barney shook his head as if to say there was no reason for concern. I turned back to the front window of the cab yet couldn't help but feel alarmed.

In front of the impressive backdrop of the House of Commons and the spire of Big Ben, a considerable crowd had gathered on Parliament Square Garden and spilled over onto Victoria Embankment. They were a mixed bunch, not just marchers, holding signs letting everyone know what had brought them out in droves. They read, 'Free Hannington', 'Free Sydney Elias' and 'Power to Labour'. Those protesters had been called by the Labour movement to free the two leaders of the marchers, Wal Hannington and Sydney Elias. Without them, the movement was like a hydra from which two heads had been cut off, but new ones failed to grow back. The Labour movement was in bad need of charismatic leaders because the riots news coverage and its violent oppression was exactly what the movement needed to gather political momentum. Without leaders to speak for them, those marchers would return to being simply a noisy, hungry crowd without political agenda.

Driving down Parliament Square took us the better part of thirty minutes. Further down, the traffic grew much lighter on our side, while the lane going in the opposite direction was clogging up and the car horns were sounding. We drove on in silence, knowing that nothing now stood between us and what would no doubt be a very unpleasant conversation.

I wondered how Barnaby felt and whether he had put handcuffs in his coat pocket. I had no family to speak off so I could barely begin to fathom how it felt like to drive to one of my own, knowing I might well have to arrest them for the worst of all possible crimes, murder.

Out of the blue, I realised that if the identity of the suspect had been known to his superiors, Barnaby would never have been allowed to make this arrest himself, let alone accompanied by a civilian, let alone in a simple taxicab. I was forced to deduce that the conclusion he and I had come to, after Constable Gray's testimony, had not been disclosed to his superiors. It also meant that no one knew where we were going, who we were interrogating and on what grounds.

With a shudder, I wondered if indeed there were handcuffs in Barnaby's coat pocket. Was there a real possibility that he might let his uncle get away, lock, stock and barrel? What if his filial love for his uncle rendered him incapable of sending the old man to jail? What if he only wanted to hear him out, listen and let him off the hook?

I calmed myself. If this was the case, he wouldn't have brought me along. And Barnaby was the most upstanding human being I knew. He was unable, no matter how much he felt for someone, of letting anything get the better of the law, let alone of murder. That probably meant me too, I pondered, remembering the evil church in Dean's Mews.

What if he had invited me yesterday out of his upstanding nature but had changed his mind during the night? He had left me that note at the oddest time. What if he had gone to Uncle Bernard to warn him and had arranged for him to vanish into the night? What if this car ride was a sham to make me believe he wanted to confront his uncle? Would I have to watch him act surprised when we found the nest empty?

So many possibilities, and few of them with good outcomes. I wanted so much to look at Barnaby to judge what was going on.

He noticed the motion of my head and gave me a reassuring smile and squeezed my hand. He had misunderstood my worried look. I didn't feel empathy anymore, it was the fear of discovering he was fallible and less of a man than I thought him to be.

What did that say about me? Did I want him to be perfect? If I wanted him to be lenient with me, why should he not be lenient with his family? All these thoughts had me quite nervous and worried. If I had felt queasy at the prospect of the conversation we were to have, I now felt downright terrified it wouldn't take place at all.

Fulham Road looked tranquil enough when we finally drove down it, heading towards the door I had seen once before. Its white buildings and black fences were the guardians of English respectability. Most people needed to feel that way, I suppose. For my part, I had witnessed and taken part in enough mischief and positively reprehensible behaviour behind those doors to know it was all for show. Wickedness could thrive anywhere, paint peeling off or not.

Finally, the cabbie halted the Austin with screeching wheels at the address Barney had given him. He helped me out of the car and paid the man. I distinctly felt him hesitate before stepping towards that door. Was it his guilty conscience or the fear for his uncle's fate? I was about to find out. We walked towards the black lacquered door hand in hand and Barnaby rung the bell.

We heard Bernard's shuffling steps coming towards us. I was instantaneously relieved by that sound. Whatever else came to pass, Bernard hadn't vanished like a thief. We watched apprehensively as the door opened. I don't know what I was expecting but I think it's fair to say that I was surprised at how calm and composed Uncle Bernard appeared. A brief glance at Barney's face let me know he also was astonished at his uncle's quiet manner. His shirt, under his jacket, was crumpled but he was otherwise his neat and trimmed self. He greeted us with a broad smile.

"Barnaby! Lucy! I am so happy to see you! Please, come in," he said with a motion of the newspaper in his hand. "What brings you here?" he asked as he walked us to the living room.

The place was not quite as tidy as it was when I had visited last time, but the changes were minute, which is more than could be said about Uncle Bernard's demeanour. He was more jovial than I ever thought him capable of.

"We were wondering how you were," Barney said as we sat down on the couch, side by side, as if we needed to support each other.

"I am fine, I am fine," Uncle Bernard laughed. "The kettle has just boiled, let me get some tea," he said with pride. He almost left the room but turned back to say, "Normally, Kate does it but, since she's not here, I think it's all right if I do the honours."

He walked quickly out of the room. I wasn't sure but I thought I heard him hum. I looked quizzically at Barney and he seemed as puzzled as me. He shrugged with his palms towards the sky.

Before I could get more out of him, Uncle Bernard came back into the room with a tray. The crockery was a haphazard collection of motives and designs. The teapot, the milk jug and the sugar pot were there so the bare essentials were covered.

"Barnaby, would you be so kind and be mother?"

Although all present knew he meant for

Barney to pour the tea, it sent a shudder down my spine and I saw Barnaby's knuckle whiten on the teapot's handle and his jaw clench.

"Of course, Uncle Bernard," he said, kindly enough.

"And you, young lady, tell me, what brought you here today?"

For a moment, I thought he was revealing to us that this had all been an act and that he knew exactly why we were there, but I saw his vacant eyes and beatific smile. This man had no idea why we were there or, much worse, he did not seem to find it strange that his wife had not come home in the last few days. Maybe he didn't know what had happened at Wellington Arch. Maybe it wasn't him after all. Still, his behaviour was odd. I decided to prod him gently.

"We wanted to see you, Uncle Bernard," I said, taking the cup and saucer Barnaby handed to me with a warning glare. Since I didn't know whether it pertained to the tea or my line of questioning, I ignored him. "How are you today?"

"I am very well, my girl, thank you. And you?"

"I am all right, thank you."

"And you, Barnaby, how are you? Do you remember when you were a boy, Kate would always fuss over you and, at the slightest cough, you would be sent to bed for days. Even if you had only swallowed a bug," he laughed.

And his laughter kept going and going. Hysteria. Unquestionably. Whether it was the shock of finding out she had died or the trauma of killing her himself, this man was in shock.

Barney and I sipped our tea, watching him in dismay, waiting for the fit to subside.

"I remember," Barnaby said calmly, when the gloomy silence had returned to the room. "How is Auntie Kate?" he asked cautiously, hiding behind his cup of tea.

"To tell the truth, I don't rightly know," he said, looking about him as if for a key or a dropped earring. "I haven't seen her in a while."

"Really? How long?" I asked with the same careful tone one uses not to frighten a stray cat.

"Truly, I don't know that either," he answered. "Isn't that silly?"

"Do you remember when you saw her last?" Barney was quick to cut in.

"No, no I don't. I have tried to," he said, shutting his eyes forcefully, aggressively searching his memories.

"Did you see her here?" Barnaby asked.

"Yes, yes, here, in the hall," Bernard said without opening his eyes. "It was early in the morning, one of her early morning appointments. Her work, she called it."

"She was in the habit of going out early?"

"Not a habit, I would say, about once a month or so."

"Did she tell you where she went?"

"Oh no," Bernard said, opening his eyes and putting his hand on Barney's knee. "You know what your aunt could be like when she felt that we were not following her instructions. Surely you remember that she was quite unnerved when we asked what she did or where she went. I have learnt that long ago, and I don't ask anymore. But that morning, just looking at her putting on her coat and taking her old Gladstone bag was too much. I asked and she had a right go at me."

He had rambled on quite rapidly, almost monotonously. He looked into the distance and seemed lost in the memories of his time with Kate. Or was he remembering what he had done to her? If that was the case, he didn't remember why because the look on his face reflected puzzlement and confusion.

"Why are you here again?" he asked, looking at Barney and me in turn.

"We wanted to make sure you're all right," Barnaby said. "Are you managing without Auntie Kate?"

"I would say I'm even enjoying it, very much," the old mad man said, settling in his armchair, putting both hands on his knees and looking at us in turn. "The evening we spent at your show, my dear girl, was quite the eye opener. I came out of that theatre a new man. I couldn't remember being this happy ever. Thank you!"

"You're welcome," I whispered, unsure what to say in consternation and the terror of what other consequences that visit to the Black Cat might have had.

"Excuse me, Uncle, but what work was Auntie Kate doing?"

"I told you. Every month or so, out comes the Gladstone, as if she is some kind of doctor, and off she goes into the wee hours of the morning and doesn't come back until lunch… or later. But always with money. I wasn't supposed to know," he added with a secretive smile, "but once, she thought I was sleeping in this very armchair when she returned from one of her outings. I peeped and saw her counting the pound notes. There were quite a few, let me tell you. Quite clever, don't you think?" he winked at us, oblivious to our looks of utter dejection.

"You knew she had money on her when she came back from those outings?" Barney asked as casually as he could.

"Why, yes, of course. I just told you."

"And you think she left for one of those appointments when you last saw her?" Barnaby asked.

"Yes, I supposed so since she took her bag with her."

"Did she take anything else? Like a suitcase?"

"A suitcase? Do you think she went to the sea without us?" he winked again.

"That would explain why she hasn't come back."

"Yes," he responded lost in thought. "Eastbourne is lovely. But not in this season. No, if she left, she must have gone some place else."

"You know what season it is?" Barney asked, fully recovered and laying his trap.

"Yes, yes, it's October so it's Autumn. And there's been a raucous in Hyde Park. The papers were full of it."

"You mean, you didn't see them for yourself?" I asked, trying to ascertain when the apparent amnesia kicked in.

"No, I keep away from any such trouble, my dear girl. I know you young people crave adventure but an old man likes his peace and quiet."

"What did Auntie Kate have to say about that

raucous?" Barnaby asked.

"Nothing," Uncle Bernard answered, searchingly. "I don't think she saw them."

"You think she's gone since before that day? The day you saw the paper that told you about the riots in Hyde Park?"

"Let me think… Yes, I was alone here, I'm sure I was."

"And how long had you been alone? A day? Half a day? Did she leave the morning of that paper? Or maybe the day before?" Barnaby asked, his questions clicking like the metal grind of a trap being stretched open, ready to close on its unknowing victim. It was almost unbearable to watch. I felt my every nerve tensing along with each question. The world outside that living room had all but vanished.

"You know what?" Uncle Bernard asked wide eyed and smiling, "I don't remember exactly. You'd think I'd remember such a thing," he sniggered and recovered. "I think it was the day before. But what difference does it make?"

"I am trying to find Auntie Kate," said Barney, "we all are. Now, if you remember receiving the paper here the day after Auntie Kate had gone off with her bag, do you remember what you did between the early morning hours when she left and the next day, around mid morning, when the postman delivered the paper?"

"That's so long ago," he moaned. "Let me think. I heard her leave…"

"You heard her? You didn't see her off?"

"No. Once I did that and she told me off. So now I stay in my room and sit on my bed until I hear her slam the door. Only then did I go downstairs and sit here and listen to the wireless or to my old records… Maybe I went to the window and watched her walk towards Earls Court, with that silly bag in her hand." His eyes grew vacant and then they found me. "Did I tell you, dear girl, I have a rather extensive collection of records."

"No, you didn't," I said, trying hard to smile and hide my dread.

"I like the sound, you see. If I hear them, it means I am home and Kate's home, taking care of me."

"But you didn't think it strange that she didn't come home? Or didn't call you to let you know she was all right?"

"No. I don't get to use the telephone. She picks it up when she's home and if I am alone, I must let it ring."

"Has it rung in the last few days?" Barney asked.

"No, it has been quiet. I like it, when it's peaceful. Maybe it was too quiet. I played my records a little louder than I am supposed to, but I needed a bit of noise."

Barnaby sighed and looked from Uncle Bernard to me. This conversation was mad, and I was out of questions. I didn't know how to get him to talk anymore about that day or about what he might have done. To be honest, I was a little frightened by the prospect of a confession. It was so difficult for me to believe that anyone, let alone Bernard, was capable of such a crime.

"The teapot is empty, Uncle Bernard," Barnaby said, matter of factly. "Let me make a fresh pot."

With that, he left the room holding the tray and gave me an encouraging nod over his shoulder. I wasn't quite sure what he expected me to do. I liked Uncle Bernard and I think he liked me back but that didn't mean he would confide in me more that he would in his nephew or to the both of us together. That's when I understood what Barney was hoping would happen. I didn't know how I was going to bring about the mood required to get more concrete information out of the old man, but I was going to try. Rational questions had not yielded much in terms of clues. Maybe a more round about, underhand approach would get some results. But those were the results I was afraid of. I wanted to believe that Bernard was innocent of that crime and I was reluctant to be the one to coax it out of him. Apparently, that was Barnaby's plan and I felt there was no arguing about it. No doubt he wasn't even in the kitchen but in the corridor, out of sight, listening to us. The responsibility weighed heavy on my shoulders and they sagged further as I drew breath before preparing my opening question.

"Are you all right, my dear girl?" Uncle Bernard inquired, moving a little closer. With that he started the conversation that was to lead him to jail. How I wish I hadn't done such a good job.

"I am all right, thank you Uncle Bernard," I said, trying to smile. "I am worried about Auntie Kate."

"Really?" he winked. "You didn't seem to like her all that much when you came here last time."

"No, no, I liked her all right. She took good care of Barney, all these years."

"That she did," he said, sighing, with a glance towards the silent kitchen. "He is the true love of her life."

I let that sentence hang in the air for Barney's

benefit as much as to give me time to come up with the next leading question.

"But she took good care of you too, right?"

"Yes, she did. The house was always spick and span and the meals were always ready on time, even if not very good," he winked in my direction and I smiled at him.

I felt dreadful, like I was serving a condemned man his last meal or offering him one last warm smile. All the same, I soldiered on. What else was there left to do?

"Do you remember what she cooked the night before she went out early?"

"Of course, some over done Irish stew. I don't like it even if it's done right but I didn't tell her that."

"There are a lot of things that you can and cannot do when she's around, isn't that so?" I winked.

"That's right, but she takes care of me."

"Haven't you felt so much more free during this last week?"

"Yes… and strangely relieved."

"Relieved about what?"

"Let me see. I remember coming through the door on Thursday afternoon, feeling a weight off my shoulder. It would be hard to tell you more than that, my dear."

My heart sank. Thursday was the day of the riots. I could hear the springs of Barney's trap slowly creaking shut. All I wanted to do was to keep them from closing in on him. That wasn't what I had come to this place to do, on that fateful Monday morning. I looked at him, trying to apologize in advance for what I was about to do, because I had to, not because I wanted to.

"Last Thursday? You went out?"

"Yes… I think… for a little while."

"Why did you go out?"

"I am not supposed to, but it was noon and I was hungry and Kate hadn't come home yet."

"So you went looking for her?"

"Yes, I think."

"Where did you go?"

"I don't remember, I am sorry."

"And you didn't find her?"

"No, I came back here, tired and hungry, but strangely relieved."

"What did you do then? Fix some lunch?"

"No. First I had to clean myself up. I don't remember what I did but my hands and sleeves were covered in black and red ink. I had to throw away the coat and shirt. I could never have explained to Kate how I got them this dirty. Once I wore a fresh shirt, I made some lunch. I was famished. I don't know where I went or how long

I was gone but I remember the clock striking four in the living room when I sat down to my platter of bangers on toast. For once, they were done the way I like them, grilled to a crisp with the toast brown on both sides."

He smiled at me like a boy with a new balloon. My stomach felt like a lump of lead and the tears were welling in my eyes. I had to keep going, there was no turning back now. I imagined Barnaby fighting back tears too in the corridor.

"What did you do with the coat and the shirt, Uncle Bernard?"

"They're in the hamper, of course. I have been sweeping but I haven't got around to the laundry yet. Actually, my dear, you couldn't lend me a hand with that, could you?"

"I'd be happy to. Where is the laundry hamper?"

"It's in the bedroom, of course."

I immediately saw Barney silently tip toe down the corridor and up the stairs. Uncle Bernard sat with his back to the hall and was beaming at me. No doubt, the Detective Inspector was going to get the evidence, maybe to convince himself that it was true or find proof it was a misunderstanding.

"Of course," I said, "I'll take it with me when

"What did you do with the coat and the shirt, Uncle Bernard?"

we go. Now, Uncle Bernard, you remember putting on your coat at noon because you were hungry and went out?"

"Yes, that I do."

"But not where you went?"

"No, strange, isn't it? I wish I did, so I could explain to Kate how my coat and shirt got so dirty."

"Maybe I can help you?"

"Could you? That would be so very nice."

"Of course. Why don't you close your eyes? That'll help you focus on the images in your head."

"Wonderful, wonderful, such a great trick," he said, clapping his hands and closing his eyes.

The timing was awfully good. Just at that moment, I saw, behind Bernard's armchair, Barney come down the stairs slowly, as if he was carrying something very heavy. In his hands, I only saw a man's coat and shirt. Much to my horror, I could make out, on the sleeves of both the shirt and the coat, dark menacing stains. They were all the more disconcerting that they were so large. How had he managed to hide them all the way home? Surely someone must have noticed that old man, leaving Hyde Park Corner, his hands awkwardly tucked under his coat? That is how I imagined he got away with it. But that was the tragedy of it all. He wasn't trying to get away from anything. He was peacefully sitting there, listening to my instructions, while his nephew, the very picture of disappointment and misery, silently leant against the doorframe. He was waiting to see whether my little experiment would get him to tell us why such a thing had to happen to all of us.

"So, it's Thursday noon, you're hungry, you've put on your coat and you're walking out the front door."

"Yes, I step out and start walking. Goodness, I just realised I forgot to lock up."

"Is hunger the only thing you're feeling?"

"I am hungry and angry that she should not be back for my meal. She's such a stickler for punctuality herself."

"That's true. You're hungry and angry. Do you go left or right when you exit the house?"

"I go left."

"You're walking up Fulham Road."

"Yes."

"How far do you walk?"

"I don't know exactly, but a long time, all the way past Harrods."

I briefly glanced towards Barney. We silently agree. He went towards Hyde Park Corner. My tall and courageous lover closed his eyes and lowered his head.

"And where to after that?"

"I don't know. I heard a lot of noise. People shouting, police whistles, horses whining. What is going on?"

"Did you see anything?"

"I must have, but I don't remember," he said, opening his eyes, smiling at me apologetically. "I am sorry, dear, it's all a blur. I only remember retracing my steps later, being tired and in a hurry to get home. I wasn't frightened she would be there. Somehow, I was more afraid that she was chasing me. Silly, isn't it?"

"Yes," I said, smiling feebly. "It's silly," I sighed. "I am so sorry, Uncle Bernard."

"Sorry about what, darling Lucy?" he asked, putting his hands on mine.

"We have to take you for a cab ride, Uncle Bernard," Barnaby said in a whisper.

"Oh! There you are, my dear boy," he said, getting up to go to his nephew. "You never brought us tea. What do you have there? Did you go through my things?"

"Yes, Uncle Bernard, I did. I had to. And now I must ask you to come with us."

"Why? Where are we going?"

"To Scotland Yard," Barney said, staring helplessly into his uncle's eyes. "You are under arrest for the murder of Katherine, your wife. Anything you say will be used in evidence in a court of law. I am sorry, uncle, more than you know."

"What? That's absurd, my boy," he said, but added nothing further.

He let himself drop on the third step, head down, eyes glazing over. Barnaby motioned for me to come over. He whispered in my ear to help Uncle Bernard with his jacket and shoes. I was glad to be moving and busy, trying not to think what the consequences of this would be. I was glad Barney didn't give me the blood-stained coat and shirt to hold while he dressed his uncle. The old man was resilient, like a child, going through the motions.

Barnaby, in the meantime, made a muted telephone call to the Yard to send a car over. Our trip to Fulham Road was a private one. The way back was official business and no cab would do to transport a suspected murderer. We waited in a distressed silence in the hall until the car arrived. We stood there, the three of us, in hats and coats, as if on display at Madame Tussauds. The small window above the door shed a gloomy light down on our lowered heads.

When the car finally halted at the given address, we left the house, Barney locking up what might soon prove to be his house, if he wanted it. me towards us looking at Bernard and me to find out who was being arrested. Barnaby had not put handcuffs on his uncle's wrists. Barnaby and Uncle Bernard and a bobby sat in the back. The other bobby sat at the wheel.

As I was about to sit down beside him, I heard Uncle Bernard ask Barney, "She's dead, isn't she?"

BASED ON FACT: THE MURDER

On 27th October 1932, 100,000 unemployed men gathered in Hyde Park Corner, having walked to the capital from every part of the UK, starting in Glasgow on 26th September. When a brick was thrown through a post office window at Great Cumberland Place, mounted police charged with clubs and rioting began, resulting in sixty to seventy injuries and numerous arrests.

THE THEATRE

The Windmill Theatre — now The Windmill International — in Great Windmill Street, London was for many years both a variety and revue theatre. The Windmill remains best known for its nude *tableaux vivants*, which began in 1932. In 1930, Laura Henderson bought the Palais de Luxe building and hired Howard Jones, an architect, to remodel the interior to a small 320-seat, one-tier theatre. It was then renamed the Windmill. It opened on 22 June 1931, as a playhouse.

These facts served as inspiration. This is a work of fiction. Names, characters, businesses, places, events and incidents are either the products of the author's imagination or used in a fictitious manner. Any resemblance to characters alive or dead is purely coincidental.

Secrets of a Dancing Girl
The Series

1. The Chess Player
2. A Mouthful of Bread
3. One of Us
4. My Lover
5. The Priest
6. Hunger March

Keep in touch at:

http://www.secretsofadancinggirl.co.uk/